Clubhouse

KIRBY'S
CIRCUS

WITHDRAWN

By Alexis Strathmann
Illustrated by Gary Krejca

BARRON'S

Table of Contents

Illustration on page 21 by Carol Stutz; Illustrations on pages 22–23 by Deborah Gross

All inquiries should be addressed to:
Barron's Educational Series, Inc.
250 Wireless Boulevard
Hauppauge, New York 11788
www.barronseduc.com

Library of Congress Catalog Card No.: 2006028821

ISBN-13: 978-0-7641-3722-8
ISBN-10: 0-7641-3722-0

Library of Congress Cataloging-in-Publication Data
Strathmann, Alexis.
 Kirby's circus / by Alexis Strathmann.
   p. cm. — (Reader's clubhouse)
 ISBN-13: 978-0-7641-3722-8
 ISBN-10: 0-7641-3722-0
 1. English language—Phonetics—Juvenile literature.
 2. Circus—Juvenile literature. I. Title.

PE1135.S77 2007
 428.1—dc22

                                                                2006028821

PRINTED IN CHINA
9 8 7 6 5 4 3 2 1

Dear Parent and Educator,

Welcome to the Barron's Reader's Clubhouse, a series of books that provide a phonics approach to reading.

Phonics is the relationship between letters and sounds. It is a system that teaches children that letters have specific sounds. Level 1 books introduce the short-vowel sounds. Level 2 books progress to the long-vowel sounds. Level 3 books then go on to vowel combinations and words ending in "y." This progression matches how phonics is taught in many classrooms.

Kirby's Circus introduces the "ir," "er," and "ur" vowel combination sound. Simple words with these vowel combinations are called **decodable words.** The child knows how to sound out these words because he or she has learned the sound they include. This story also contains **high-frequency words.** These are common, everyday words that the child learns to read by sight. High-frequency words help ensure fluency and comprehension. **Challenging words** go a little beyond the reading level. The child may need help from an adult to understand these words. All words are listed by their category on page 24.

Here are some coaching and prompting statements you can use to help a young reader read *Kirby's Circus*:

- **On page 4, "Circus" is a decodable word. Point to the word and say:**

  Read this word. How did you know the word? What sounds did it make?

  Note: There are many opportunities to repeat the above instruction throughout the book.

- **On page 5, "giraffe" is a challenging word. Point to the word and say:**

  Read this word. Sound out the word. How did you know the word? What helped you?

You'll find more coaching ideas on the Reader's Clubhouse Web site: *www.barronsclubhouse.com*. Reader's Clubhouse is designed to teach and reinforce reading skills in a fun way. We hope you enjoy helping children discover their love of reading!

Sincerely,

Nancy Harris

Nancy Harris
Reading Consultant

Have you ever been to Kirby's Circus? Here's what you will see at Kirby's Circus.

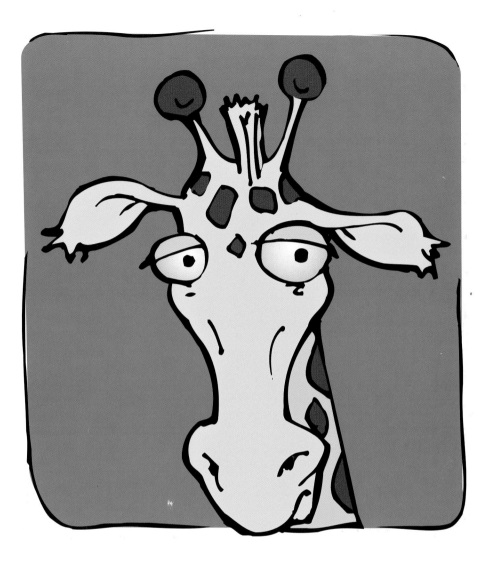

Did you ever see a giraffe at a circus?

Come to Kirby's Circus. You
can see a herd of giraffes with
purple spots. Kirby's giraffes
can climb up ladders.

Did you ever see a turtle at a circus?

Come to Kirby's Circus. You
can see turtle drivers. Kirby's
turtles drive around in
sweaters.

Did you ever see a beaver at a circus?

Come to Kirby's Circus. You can see Bertha the brown beaver. Kirby's beaver likes this dress made of glitter.

Did you ever see a squirrel at a circus?

Come to Kirby's Circus. You
can see Murphy the squirrel.
Kirby's squirrel can surf in
circles.

Did you ever see a tiger at a circus?

Come to Kirby's Circus. You
can see a tiger named Tyler.
Kirby's tiger likes to take
showers.

Did you ever see a butterfly at a circus?

Come to Kirby's Circus. You
can see Irving the butterfly.
Kirby's butterfly likes to show off
his good manners.

Now would you like to see the master of Kirby's Circus?

Here is Kirby!

Kirby always has a surprise or two at his circus.

Fun Facts About CIRCUSES

- A clown at a circus is called a "Joey."

- There are many circuses in the United States. Peru, Indiana, has had more circuses than anywhere else in the United States.

- Some circus people believe that finding peacock feathers brings bad luck.

- The Ringling Brothers circus has 55 elephants. Every year, it spends more than $6 million to take care of them.

• Some big circuses are "three-ring" circuses. Performers do different kinds of acts at the same time. They happen in three different rings on the stage. The "ringmaster" runs the show. The ringmaster announces all the acts.

audience

ring one

ringmaster

ring two

ring three

Paper Circus Parade

Some circuses arrive at a town with a circus parade. In this activity, you can make your own circus parade.

You will need:
- colored construction paper
- safety scissors
- glue
- markers, crayons, or colored pencils
- wide wooden craft sticks

1. Draw the outlines of your favorite circus animals. Use a marker or crayon. You can draw any animal you like.

2. Use safety scissors to cut out the animals. Color in the animals' features. Use a marker or crayon.

3. Glue a wooden craft stick to the back of each animal. Be sure to glue only the top half of the stick to the paper.

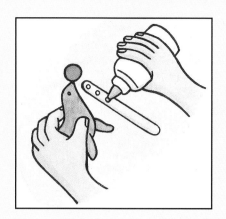

4. Make several animals. Then you can have a circus parade. Do this activity with friends. You can have a really long parade!

Word List

Challenging Words

giraffe
giraffes
squirrel

Decodable ir, er, & ur Words

beaver	glitter	master	tiger
Bertha	herd	Murphy	turtle
butterfly	Irving	purple	turtles
circles	Kirby	showers	Tyler
circus	Kirby's	surf	
drivers	ladders	surprise	
ever	manners	sweaters	

High-Frequency Words

a	dress	made	to
always	good	named	two
and	has	now	up
around	have	of	walk
at	here	off	what
been	here's	or	will
brown	his	see	would
can	in	show	you
climb	is	take	
come	like	the	
did	likes	this	

7